Tenshi

Cheyenne Reed

PublishAmerica
Baltimore

© 2012 by Cheyenne Reed.
All rights reserved. No part of this book may be reproduced, stored in a retrieval system or transmitted in any form or by any means without the prior written permission of the publishers, except by a reviewer who may quote brief passages in a review to be printed in a newspaper, magazine or journal.

First printing

All characters in this book are fictitious, and any resemblance to real persons, living or dead, is coincidental.

PublishAmerica has allowed this work to remain exactly as the author intended, verbatim, without editorial input.

Softcover 9781462685424
PUBLISHED BY PUBLISHAMERICA, LLLP
www.publishamerica.com
Baltimore

Printed in the United States of America

Tenshi

Cheyenne Reed

I want to thank:
Colin Browne, Rachel Lewis, Liyox16 on deviantart.com and Galidor the Dragon on deviantart.com!
Thank you so much for letting me use your characters!

Contents

Chapter One: Nightmare 7
Chapter Two: First Day 13
Chapter Three: "Knock, knock" Said the Wolf 19
Chapter Four: First Encounter 25
Chapter Five: Embarrassment 29
Chapter Six: The Assumed Date 34
Chapter Seven: The Attack Begins 44
Chapter Eight: Deceived 53
Chapter Nine: The Battle 57
Chapter Ten: Kidnapped 65

Chapter One: Nightmare

"They are after me!" a young cat spirit cried "Please somebody help! Anybody! Just please don't let them kill me!" she was running as fast as she could to get away, but they were faster, the wolves were gaining on her; the alpha was fierce and cunning, leading them to their dinner.

"You two speed up and take the sides..." The alpha ordered "I'll take the lead." She grinned a big toothy grin.

"Right." One subordinate replied increasing his speed.

"As always Ma'am." The other replied smiling with her, also increasing his speed.

"Why are you doing this?!" The cat cried again "Why me?...Why My family?!"

The alpha's two subordinates answered in unison "Because you are the cat and canines always EAT the cat." They laughed the most malicious laugh that the cat had ever heard; the alpha jumped in front of her prey stopping the cat dead in her tracks.

"My family has done you no wrong or harm..." the cat was crying hard now "Why did you kill them?" She was pleading for an answer and the alpha answered in a calm terrifying voice.

"Because... We were hungry"

The cat stood in petrified horror; the alpha attacked her poor, defenseless prey slashing at her throat, but missing because of her squirming.

"Hold still you little brat!" The alpha took another strike slicing a deep gash across the cat's chest, she screamed in agony; the alpha's subordinates came in from the sides and began cutting the cat's arms making her bleed profusely.

"STOP!!" The cat screamed, but no one listened; the alpha struck for the cat's throat again.

I sat up screaming sweat making my clothes cling to my skin, hair sticking to my face I was soaked, my hand was at my throat the scar protruding from the rest of my skin; my mind thought back to that fateful day all the blood, I started to cry. *Why is it always that dream?* I thought to myself; as I cried I felt cool hands resting on my shoulders.

"Shinra...?" I heard a man's voice say, "Shinra what's wrong?!" I looked up at the man trying to soothe my agonized tears; he had black hair, cat ears and a tail to match, his eyes were bright silver and at times they were cold as ice, but not now. Right now he was trying to save me, again, from my memories.

"Ikuto!" I screamed wrapping my arms around him and crying into his shoulder.

"Shhh, it's ok…" He said wrapping his arms around my waist and rocking me back and forth soothingly, his voice soft.

"Nothing is going to hurt you… Not while I'm here to protect you." He whispered trying to calm my fears. I thought back to that painful memory; it was storming the thunder ringing in my ears, the smell of blood overwhelmed my nose, the sight of the wolf pack swarming for the kill, the fear that death was upon me, the smell of the rain everything is so clear and so terrifying. I trembled and Ikuto held me tighter; a few minutes passed and my tears were starting to recede as I pulled my head away from his shoulder, only to see a scar on it. It was a large scar from a wolf bite it was pinkish in color with a hint of red in the center where the teeth penetrated deeply, the scar wrapped around his shoulder almost like a tattoo; I started to wonder if he had slept at all, but I was too afraid to ask, so I simply asked what time it was.

"It's around two in the morning Shinra... This is the longest you've slept in a while." Ikuto said smiling; I looked up to see, unfortunately, the bags under his eyes had darkened. I knew he hadn't slept.

"I kept you up didn't I?"I asked sadly looking down.

"Not at all..." Ikuto replied reaching behind him to grab a book "I couldn't sleep so I have been catching up on my reading." He gave me his famous crooked smile and he looked so cute I couldn't stay sad; I gave him a hug and held him tightly.For some reason I had failed to realize that being able to see his scar meant Ikuto was shirtless.

I felt my face turn bright red, the heat rising in my cheeks; I squeaked hiding my head in my pillows and covering my face with my blanket.

"What is it Shinra?" Ikuto asked laughing; I looked at him and stuck out my tongue, because he knew exactly what was wrong now.

"Shinra I hate to tell you this, but... You are beet red." He laughed again.

"Gee! I wonder why?!" I hissed pointing at his bare chest.

"What?..." He grinned "This?" Ikuto leaned over the bed I was sitting on; he was lying across my lap and rolled over so he was facing the ceiling. All I could do was blush uncontrollably at how cute he looked, just like a black house cat "I-Ikuto?" I asked, *I stuttered! I can't believe I Stuttered!* I thought to myself.

"Yes Shinra?" Ikuto asked, laughing again; I couldn't answer I was too busy watching his muscle flex as he laughed, turning more and more red as I watched.

"Shinra... Are you gandering at me?!" he said pretending to be insulted.

"NO!" I almost screamed, my face as red as it could be; Ikuto rolled back onto his stomach and lay next to me. Ikuto wrapped his arms around me pulling me close, as soon as my chest touched his he giggled and blushed.

"What?" I asked feeling stupid at my question, because I knew *"what"*.

"Nothing." Ikuto said smiling and pulling me closer.

"You need sleep you know." I told him, accepting his embrace and embraced him as well.

"Yes, but so do you." He said resting his head on the pillows "Tomorrow… Well, today is a big day for you."

"Really… Why?" I said starting to fall asleep again.

"Because you start school today." Ikuto rubbed my head like I was a child.

"I do… Don't I?"

"Yes you do…" That was the last thing I heard him say, until he was screaming for me to get up; I decided that since he was screaming it was time to get up and let the day start on its path. The room was filled with sunlight as I opened my eyes, the sudden light stinging my darkness loving eyes slightly. I rolled out of bed and walked to my folding door closet standing with my back to the sun as I looked inside to see what Ikuto had bought me the day before for school. As soon as I saw what he bought I swore to myself he would NEVER buy my clothes again; what I saw was a miniature blue plaid skirt, which would most likely show my butt if I bent over, a red tank top, that was in my opinion cut way to low, a sleeveless light blue jacket that reached the bottom hem of the skirt and a red collar with a bright yellow bell on it. I sighed with frustration at his odd form of fashion and walked into the kitchen where Ikuto had cooked breakfast, I could smell the bacon that had sizzled in a hot pan not long before I woke up.

"Ikuto... can I wear a pair of your jeans?" I asked pouting at him.

"Why? Don't the clothes I bought fit you?" He asked a grin on his face.

"Yes but..." I tried to think of something corny to say to make him blush as payback for last night, "But I really like your scent..." Just as I planned his face started turning red and he turned around.

"Fine" he said quickly as his voice cracked "Which pair do you want?"

"Why don't you pick them... they are yours' after all." I said giving it a little bit of childish indecision; Ikuto turned around and headed to our room, walking to his side of the room and his closet. He grabbed a pair of jeans and tossed them to me.

"Do those work?" his face was still down and very red; I giggled at his embarrassment.

"Yes very much. Now, out so I can change." Ikuto passed by me and left the room mumbling something to himself; I unfolded the jeans Ikuto had tossed me, they were a pair of wranglers long and faded.

I took off my pajamas and put on the jeans they covered my feet and sagged down to my hips, Ikuto is 6'4 I am a messily 5'4 so they are huge on me, I put on the tank top, it wasn't as low as I thought it would be, I put on the collar then the pair of shoes Ikuto had bought; I looked in the mirror and noticed the collar covered my scar, Ikuto was looking out for me again. He knew I hated people starring at my scars especially the one on my neck, people would always come up and ask if I had tried to kill myself; I smiled and put on the jacket, unfortunately it didn't cover the scars on my arms, but that was ok I could deal with being called 'emo' or a 'cutter' because I knew those were in no way true. I fixed my mess of hair and headed to the kitchen.

"You ready Ikuto... Oops! I mean Mr. Kanasai." I poked at him playfully; he had put on his glasses so he really did look like a teacher.

"Yes I am... Are you?" Ikuto poked my shoulder and I turned showing him I was as ready as I could be.

"Then let's go." Ikuto said smiling and led me out the door.

Chapter Two: First Day

The sun was shining through the windows of the foyer above the school's main entrance way and I stood mesmerized at the beautiful stained glass windows; the colors caused by the shining light was so amazing. The bell rang and I realized it was two minutes before first period started. I was running no sprinting is more the word; I was searching for room 215 a Dr. Kamimura's class room running up flights of stairs and back down again. Looking through the numbers and names above the doors *oh my god! So many doors!* 200 Mrs. Powers, 202 Mrs. Stice, 204 Mr. Kanasai… "I can ask Ikuto!" I almost shouted; I walked into room 204 and looked around, everywhere I looked there were desks and piles of books; you could smell the scent of old books in the air, so crisp yet so molded it was almost palpable. I looked around for his ears and, sure enough, there he was at his desk looking so professional; I was so relieved I found him and walked up behind Ikuto giving hugging him around the shoulders.

"Ikuto I'm so happy I found you… I need your help." I said releasing him from the hug.

"Why what's wrong?" he almost jumped out of his chair, I pouted at him.

"I'm kind of… sort of… lost…" I looked up into his eyes as he started laughing.

"Ha-ha Shinra you came running to me because you were lost?" He smiled widely and rubbed the top of my head "That's so cute." *Ikuto called me cute?! Seriously?!*

I knew I was blushing then whenever he treated me like this I felt like such a child compared to him; I gasped and grabbed his hand remembering we were in a classroom filled with non-tardy students; I hid behind Ikuto not wanting the kids in the room to stare at me anymore than they already had been.

"Um... Iku-... I-I mean Mr. Kanasai can you tell me where this room is?" I handed him the sheet of paper that had my schedule on it, as Ikuto looked at it his eyes widened slightly.

"Ikuto... what is it?" I asked so curious to his expression.

"It's just... never mind you'll find out soon enough..." his face was sad, yet so angry, when he said this to me, "Your class is down the hall and to the right..." His eyes looked so angry, I wondered what was wrong, but I could just ask him later.

Ding Dong Ding Dong

"AH! My class is going to start! See ya Ikuto." I yelled running out the door.

"Bye Shinra." I heard him answer back; the class was in an uproar asking how Mr. Kanasai knew me.

"Gotta hurry." I told myself sprinting, again, down the hall and around the corner, my bell jingling all the way; my class was the first door, so being me, I ran into the open door on accident. I stumbled backward and landed on my butt rubbing my forehead where the door had hit me; I heard the class erupt in laughter and I saw one boy pointing at me. *OH NO! THEY SAW THAT!* I felt my face go a bright red, I noticed a strange smell in the air one I had not smelled in a long time... *A smell of wolf.*

I didn't move I was frozen my eyes going wide as the smell got more and more overwhelming; a shadow was over me and I looked up to see what seemed like a teacher. She had long blonde hair pulled up into a pony tail and blue eyes that seemed piercing and full of knowledge; I saw her ears and tail, they were just like the ones from back then. I didn't say or do anything I just starred at her; she was looking over her glasses at me.

"Well are you alright?" she asked.

"..." Nothing was said from my mouth even though I wanted to scream.

"...Are you deaf?" she asked reaching for my ear, I flinched.

"What's the matter?"

"W-w-... wolf..." I shakily pointed at her; the teacher looked confused then smiled a big grin.

"What... you got a problem with it?" she snapped her mouth shut close to my finger and I flinched again; I felt something go down my cheek and my sight was going blurry, I was crying. Crying in front of everyone in my class; *what is wrong with me? She's a teacher I shouldn't worry about it*, I thought to myself, unfortunately that isn't how it played out. The teacher noticed I was crying and reached toward me; I jumped to my feet and ran as fast as I could, *I think the last time I ran this fast was, well, that day eleven years ago.*

"HEY!" I heard the teacher yell down the hallway; I didn't look back I couldn't, I heard her yell something else, but I didn't understand her. I passed by Ikuto's room, but didn't stop I just kept running; images going through my head, the blood the torture, *I don't want that to happen again.* There were footsteps behind me getting closer and closer I tried to run faster as the scent of wolf became stronger; the tennis shoes Ikuto had gotten me were so heavy, they were hard to walk in let alone run in. The footsteps were right behind me now; I looked behind me, which was so stupid, as I did so I tripped over the heavy boots and fell flat on my face. The footsteps stopped and I heard laughter, a man's laugh coming from behind me.

"Well aren't you the graceful one." He said laughing harder.

I looked behind me and there he was; he had brown hair and blue eyes, his ears and tail were like the teacher's.

"Y-you're… you're a…. a…" I stuttered pointing at him; he stopped laughing and looked at me confused by my actions.

"I'm a what?" he asked seeming confused.

"w-w-wolf…" I was completely terrified *what would he do, no, what will he do to me?*

"Yes, and that's a problem because….?" He made hand motions and I flinched away, tears rolling down my cheeks.

"Hey… What's wrong?" he got down and kneeled in front of me; I was eye to eye with this boy. His sapphire eyes had no hatred, anger, or malicious intent; he seemed completely innocent, but it could have been my wishful thinking.

"You're… gonna…." My tears were turning into sobs and gasps that I couldn't control; he reached to put his hand on my shoulder, but stopped. I hadn't noticed my collar had fallen off, the one that concealed that dreadful, atrocious scar; this boy was now staring at my pink disgusting scar that sat in the middle of my throat.

"What… happened?" His hand moved toward my neck; I flinched and his motion stopped. "A wolf… did this…" he sounded shocked and appalled realizing why I was so terrified.

"I… have to… go…" I said between my sobs getting up from the floor; the boy just sat there he didn't follow me like before. I ran and ran as fast as I could trying to get to the dorms, I wanted Ikuto I wanted to be home; I opened the double doors that lead to our dorm and I heard Ikuto's voice.

"I told you about her past yet you still put her in Kenran's class!" he screamed; I had never heard him so angry.

"It is a class necessary for graduation I had no choice." A woman said calmly.

"No choice! You could have postponed Kenran's class until

next year! After she had the chance to adjust to the wolves here!"

"MR. KANASAI!" the woman screamed, she sounded so much scarier than Ikuto. "I assure you it's not as bad as it seems." her voice calmed.

"Not as bad as it seems…She ran out of the room crying; I saw her pass my door." He said restricting his voice so he wouldn't yell again; I needed Ikuto so badly, I needed him to hold me in his arms and tell me everything was ok.

"If that is the case then she has a detention to serve." The woman said her voice still calm; I couldn't wait any longer I ran through the doors and wrapped my arms around Ikuto burying my face in his shirt.

"Shinra…" Ikuto sounded concerned, but relieved, he wrapped his arms around me and held me tightly; I felt safe, finally safe. I kept crying and crying ruining his silk shirt.

"I-Ikuto…" I sobbed "T-t-there were…" he ran his fingers through my hair and held me.

"Shhh, it's ok." Ikuto said in a calm soothing voice, the door shut behind us; he took my hand and led me to the couch. Ikuto sat me down and kneeled in front of me; he cupped my face and looked me straight in the eyes letting me see how pained his silver eyes had become.

"I'm so sorry… I should have warned you." his eyes were so sad, I tried to stop my tears for Ikuto's sake.

"It's ok…"

"No, it's not… I should have…" He looked away, I felt his hands start to tremble; Ikuto took his hands from my face and clenched them at his sides.

"Ikuto…" I didn't know what to do or say; I tapped his shoulder trying to get his attention, he didn't look at me.

"Ikuto?" I moved in front of him and put my hand on his

cheek, I found out his soft cheeks were wet and I caressed his face in my hands.

"Ikuto… I told you it's ok." I kissed his forehead and he put his hands on my waist.

"I swear to you it's ok…" I said trying to calm him; Ikuto looked into my eyes moving his hands from my waist, over my shoulder, and to my face caressing it like a fragile piece of fine pottery.

He was leaning in, like he was going to kiss me when a knock came to the door.

Chapter Three: "Knock, knock" Said the Wolf

There was a knock at the door and Ikuto was leaning closer to me, I could feel my cheeks getting hotter and hotter as he leaned in like he was going to kiss me; the knock continued, not stopping.

"I-Ikuto…" I whimpered he looked in my eyes not wavering in his movements.

"I know… Just one…" He said as his lips brushed mine, the knocking didn't stop without answer to the door.

"Ikuto…" I said in a small breathless sigh at the small brush our lips had done; Ikuto's hand moved from my face to my neck and stopped.

"Where is your collar?" he asked as his eyes, finally, released from mine and wondered down to my neck.

"It must ha-.." The door swung open with a loud bang before I could complete my sentence.

"I said Knock Knock!!!" yelled a boy as he had kicked in the door; Ikuto jumped up standing in front of me protectively, I screamed and grabbed for his hand.

"What are you doing here?" Ikuto hissed as his ears went back defensively; I suddenly noticed a strong scent of wolf and peeked around Ikuto to see who it was who had broken into the room.

"Hey…That's the boy from before." I said timidly behind Ikuto pointing my finger shakily at him, no one had heard my small voice.

"Um… I came to return your daughter's collar." The boy said in an innocent voice as he was holding up the red collar I had been wearing earlier, it jingled at the movement; Ikuto slumped over and spoke angrily yet hurt at the same time,

"My.... Daughter?"

The boy looked down at me with a goofy grin on his face, "There you are!" he swiftly walked over to me and I flinched backwards away from him.

"Yep, it's you alright." The boy was coming closer when Ikuto stopped him abruptly.

"I don't believe I invited you in." Ikuto hissed, still sounding very protective and angry.

"Oh! My apologies." He bowed respectfully, it seemed like he knew what he was doing, he was so formal; Ikuto sighed and grabbed the bowing boy's cheek.

"Shinta what did I tell you about bowing... And she isn't my daughter."

"So... his name is Shinta..." I whispered to myself feeling my cheeks turn a little red; Shinta was really cute now that I examined him more closely.

"Sorry, sorry I was bringing back your lover's collar." Shinta said squinting at Ikuto's grip; I saw Ikuto turn red at the statement.

"She isn't my lover either!!"

Shinta sighed and looked at Ikuto, "Then what is she to you?... I'm so confused."

"She's uh... My..." Ikuto stuttered and stumbled over himself looking for the right words "She's my... Student?... Yeah... She's my student!"

Shinta looked around the room, after Ikuto had released his cheek.

"Then why is she living with you?"

I laughed at the two of them and Shinta looked down at me smiling, "So you can laugh." He swiftly moved around Ikuto and sat in front of me holding out my collar.

"I believe this is yours."

I nodded, but noticed Shinta was staring at my neck again, I covered my scar quickly.

"Could you..." I couldn't say it, but I had to.

"Shinta could you not stare at it?" Shinta averted his eyes so he was looking into mine and gestured to me apologetically.

"I'm sorry... It's just... I've never seen anyone... Live..." Shinta was looking for a proper way to put his words; Ikuto interjected, sounding annoyed, saying what Shinta meant for him, "You've never seen someone survive that kind of attack."

"Never?" I rubbed my neck where the scar stuck out from my skin, "I almost didn't..."

"How did..." Shinta sounded puzzled and confused, "Why would..."

"Why would they?" Ikuto moved around Shinta and I; he sat sloppily on the couch.

"They told Shinra it was because they were hungry." I looked away and ran my hand down my arm, my fingers passing over the scars like speed bumps.

"They tortured me and my family..."

I bit my lip holding back the tears that wanted so badly to flow again; I felt a hand on my own and looked up to see Shinta with a tormented look on his face.

"They did this too?..." He said running his fingers gently down my arm.

"They did more than that." Ikuto said bitterly "They made her watch-"

"Ikuto..." I said grabbing his pants leg; I couldn't let him continue I didn't want to remember that horrible memory. Ikuto placed his hand on my head and ran his fingers through my hair softly.

"Sorry Shinra..." Ikuto sounded sad again.

"Made her watch? Watch what?" Shinta asked, he sounded

so interested in my history; I took a deep breath and got ready to relive the worst moments of my life.

"They made me watch... as they killed my family." I said looking up at him with my head tilted, my last defense against the tears now starting to run down my cheeks; Shinta's eyes seemed to widen and sadden at the same time, he reached towards me, but I flinched again.

"So that's why you flinch whenever mama or I try to touch you." Shinta pulled his hand back and looked at it.

"I can assure you not all wolves are that malicious and blood thirsty."

"She knows that... It's just when she sees or smells a wolf she..." Ikuto looked down at me as I cried and trembled at the horrifying memories in my head, "She goes back to being five..." I gripped his leg for dear life as the images from that day as they came back over and over"...And terrify her all over again." I started crying harder as the details became clearer and clearer in the bloody pictures.

"And you just made her remember the worst part of it all..." Ikuto ran his fingers through my hair trying to calm me and he looked at Shinta with a very hatful look; pictures of my mother, my father, my brother and my grandmother came into my head one by one. Their blood coating the floor filling every nook and cranny, every crack of our kitchen; remembering was torture enough.

"I begged them... I begged them to stop..." I thought about how slowly my family had died, the screaming and the noises their wounds made, "...To leave us be and... and go away but..." Saying anything else became impossible as my tears turned to sobs.

"I'm sorry... I wish this hadn't happened to you but..." Shinta's voice was saddened, but still he sounded intrigued,

"How did you survive?"

I waited a few moments to tell him as I caught my breath and my tears began to fade.

"I played dead so they would leave me alone... when they went back to my house I tried to crawl away..." Ikuto wiped the rest of my tears away and looked at Shinta.

"I found her basically dead from blood loss, but..." I looked in Ikuto's eyes begging him to not talk anymore and he did not say anything more about it "Somehow she survived and that's all that matters..." Shinta seemed curious with the next words he spoke.

"How did you save her... from such a fate as death if she was so close?"

"I took her to my house and my parents patched up her wounds and let her rest..." Ikuto looked at me with a small smile, "She was so small it was easy to carry her... even if I was ten."

Shinta looked at Ikuto almost as if he was dumbfounded, "You carried her to your home?... And your parents didn't mind taking care of her?"

Ikuto just looked at him confused "Why wouldn't they? It was a defenseless little girl they couldn't say no." Shinta sighed and looked at me "Even so why would they put themselves through that? I mean after you they must have said no more kids." Shinta laughed to himself a little.

"WHAT IS THAT SUPPOSE TO MEAN?!" Ikuto hissed his cat ears now laying against his black hair angrily; watching the two of them bicker at each other made me laugh softly. Shinta and Ikuto looked at me confused and their bickering stopped.

"You two act like you're brothers." I laughed a little more as they stared at me both raising an eyebrow at the same time.

"We do not." They said in complete unison and all I could do was laugh more.

"See!" I pointed at them and accordingly they both blushed.

"I-I'm going to go now..." Shinta placed my collar on the table and turned to leave.

"Ok bye Shinta-sama." I said as I laughed still, Shinta stopped and looked back at me.

"S-Sama?" His face was turning a bright crimson color as he stuttered.

"Yep hehe you is a sama!" I gave him a big goofy smile and he smiled back softly as he turned back to the doors he had kicked in.

"Bye Shinta." Ikuto said smiling as he left and then looked at me "What's so funny Shinra?" I kept giggling and couldn't reply, "Come on tell me." He said smiling.

"It reminds me of a family." Ikuto smiled sweetly at me and hugged me tightly.

"Get some sleep Shinra."

"But I'm not tired." I yawned slightly.

"Yeah sure you aren't." Ikuto rolled his eyes at me and laid me against his chest.

"I'm not..." I yawned "I swear."

"Goodnight Shinra."

"Nighty night... Ikuto." My eyes closed and soon darkness consumed me.

Chapter Four: First Encounter

I woke with a fright, thunder booming outside, and the rain hitting the window like small pebbles tapping against it; the thunder roared loudly. I jumped, grabbing the blanket beside me, ran into the kitchen and hid under the kitchen table and blanket; outside the windows was pitch blackness and no light was coming through except the lightning that flashed. I couldn't tell if it was day or night.

"Ikuto?" I whimpered flinching at the thunder outside my window.

"Ikuto?!" I cried, but to my dismay no one answered; the thunder was still roaring and booming outside scaring me, making me curl up under the blanket and tremble; the menacing noise forcing me to remember the sounds and smells from long ago.

"IKUTO?!" I cried again, but the only thing that answered was the thunder and a knock on the door; the knock sounded deep like someone was using a sledge hammer to hit the door. I was paralyzed by the thunder so I watched the door and noticed something green on the counter; after focusing on the green thing I realized it was a new katana.

"Why is that there?" I asked myself out loud; just then the door busted open and at first I hoped it was Ikuto or Shinta, but I was dead wrong.

In my door way was something I had never seen before; it had black wings and three toes on each foot, it looked like something out of a sci-fi horror movie. Staying as still as I could so the creature in front of me didn't find out I was there; it walked around the room, the creature seemed to be looking for something. The thunder once again rumbled outside flinching slightly my foot knocked over a chair; the creature stopped and turned in my direction.

"Oh no..." I whispered to myself, not thinking about the consequences it may cause; this thing walked to the table I was hiding under and stopped. I tried to crawl backwards away from the approaching scent of blood and graveyard soil; there was a tapping sound above my head and I looked up, but nothing was there. I looked back in front of me and I saw pitch black eyes, teeth extending over a pair of red lips and horns which reached over and above the table; I couldn't move as my eyes widened in terror, the eyes were like staring at nothingness like looking into a black hole that wanted to swallow me whole.

It was reaching towards me, the nails on the creature's hands were long and sharp; I inched back further and knocked over two more chairs, as I inched back even further my back hit something hard and I started to cry.

"Not again..." My eyes wide with fear the creature began to stand; he looked seven feet tall at least. I looked around for something to defend myself and spotted the green katana, it was the closest thing I could reach; the creature saw me look at the katana and smiled at me.

"You think you can reach it before I slice you up?" its voice was raspy and high pitched, sounding like nails on a chalk board the noise sent shivers down my spine; I shakily stood up and my hands slid over the counter, the creature lunged for me claws out. I grabbed the katana quickly and swung it aimlessly my eyes closed tightly; something warm splattered on my hands and face. A loud thud echoed through the room and a scream followed right after, I didn't realize the scream was my own; the smell of blood intensified and became unbearable. I crumbled to the floor the katana gripped tightly in my hands;

Shinta ran into the room his hand on his sword ready to draw it and fight.

"Where's the…" Shinta stopped when he saw the body lying motionless on the floor; Shinta walked over to it and saw me in the corner the sword shaking with my own trembling hands.

"Shinra-chan?" He said coming close to me.

"Stay away!" I swung the sword wildly and Shinta grabbed its blade, I felt it slice his hand.

"Shinra-chan!" He almost screamed at me, "Shinra-chan look at me." He took his other hand and placed it softly on my cheek; I did as I was told and looked in his concerned, sad, blue eyes.

"Shi-Shinta…" I let go of the katana letting the handle drop to the floor and gripped his shirt burring my face in it as I cried harder and harder; Shinta sat still for a moment then dropped the katana and held me close to him.

"Shinra-chan." Was all he said, nothing more and nothing less; I wrapped my arms around him still crying like a small child and I felt something smear across my face. I released Shinta and looked at my arms and hands; they were covered in bright red blood.

"B…Bl-…" my mouth didn't want to work, the words wouldn't come out; I put two and two together and realized that if this was what was on my hands then it was the liquid on my face. I looked at Shinta's shirt where my face had been and saw a perfect imprint of my cheek.

"Shinra-chan?" Shinta asked sounding confused.

"T-there's… b-bl…" My mouth and brain were so off key; my brain was screaming and shouting *There's blood! There's blood!* But my mouth could barely move.

"Shinra!" Ikuto yelled as he ran into the room, my head

turned to the door way, but my mind was hazy and confused.

"I-Ikuto... t-the... b-..Bl-.." I tried to tell him, but his eyes just widened as he looked at me.

"Shinra... did you... What happened?" I raised my hands up to him trying to show him my hands, Shinta just stared at me and Ikuto.

"B-blood..." was the only word passing from my brain to my mouth successfully, I tried to stand and stumbled slightly as my mind gave way for a split second; I took a wobbly step towards Ikuto, but he stepped away from me.

"Why are you backing away?" Shinta said in my defense, sounding surprised; I took another shaky step forward and Ikuto, again, took a step back.

"I-Ikuto..." I was fighting to stay awake.

"Shi-Shinra... w-what..." Ikuto looked so afraid, so afraid of me.

"I-..." Things went black as I fell forward into the puddle of blood that had spread across the floor; I couldn't feel anything, or see anything my mind just gave out in exhaustion and shock.

Chapter Five: Embarrassment

My eyes were still shut, but I could smell blood and wolf; I shot up and looked around,light was now filling the room; ever window was open and the light of the sun was soothing and made me feel so warm and almost happy. It was in this state of relief I noticed that the monster was gone, Ikuto was gone and Shinta was sitting in a chair next to me.

"Shinra-chan... Are you ok?" he asked his eyes staring at me concerned.

"Where's the monster? Where is Ikuto?" I looked down, my hands were clean and I wasn't wearing my clothes anymore.

"Th- they're... yours..." I stuttered looking back up at him "Shinta... Why am I wearing your clothes?!"

"Yeah... yours where bl-... dirty..." he looked down "What would you like for breakfast?" he took my hand and led me to the kitchen.

"Uh... I'm not sure... Shinta?" I was so confused I barely knew this guy, but he wanted to cook me breakfast.

"Nani?" He grabbed a skillet and opened the refrigerator door.

"What..." How do I ask *what the hell happened last night?!* Shinta looked at me, he seemed to know what I was thinking, and he gave me a concerned look.

"Shinra-chan... Last night... you encountered a demon." he was so blunt when he eventually did get to the point.

"A... A demon?? Why the hell did a demon come here?!?!?!"

"He was probably looking for someone powerful, like Dr. Uzayaki." He finally let go of my hand turned around and looked out the window. "I wonder how he got past all the shields and barriers...?" he said to himself. He suddenly looked at me and said "Let's go out instead; I'm a lousy cook..." scratching the back of his head with a cute goofy grin spread across his face.

"O-ok..." *Wait... Wait...* I thought, *Go out!? Did he just ask to go out?! No, I must have heard him wrong* I nodded my head agreeing with myself.

"Alright." He said misunderstanding my nod. "Where do you want to go?"

"I'm not sure... I've never been anywhere outside the school grounds." I looked down feeling embarrassed then I realized HOW THE HELL DID I GET MY CLOTHES CHANGED IF I WAS OUT COLD!!!! I looked up glaring at Shinta "Shinta.... How did you change my Clothes?!"

"Uuuhhh..." He said, now turning a bright crimson red color. "Why don't we go to Ryan's to eat?" He said quickly changing the subject.

"NO! Before we go anywhere YOU are going to tell me HOW THE HELL YOU CHANGED MY CLOTHES!" I felt my face go more red thinking of what might have transpired.

"Well..." He couldn't look me in the eye. "I, uh... changed your clothes myself..." He was beet red as he confessed. "I would have gotten a female to do it instead, but Dr. Kamimura and Dr. Uzayaki where both busy and I don't know anyone else..." He was messing with his fingers looking down and around the room, but never at me. I wrapped my arms around myself feeling my face go an even brighter shade of red.

"D-...Did you change anything other than my top layer?" I asked looking away hoping he would say no.

"No, I have more respect than that and that didn't have bl-... dirt on it." Finally looking me in the eyes; then he bowed formally "Please forgive me."

I looked at Shinta and took a few steps forward stopping

just a few inches in front of him; I caressed his face with my hands raising his head.

"It's ok Shinta...." I looked him in the eyes "Please don't bow to me ok, you have no reason to I'm not royalty."

"I know, it's just polite." There were a few moments of silence and then he said "Shall we go now?..." I looked down at the clothes I was wearing and blushed again. "You wouldn't mind if I changed first... Would you?"

"Go ahead." Shinta said smiling.

"Thank you" I ran into my room and shut the door, I walked over to my closet and looked inside; again the only thing I had at the moment was what Ikuto had bought me so I changed, putting on the skirt and the tank top then the jacket. I examined myself in the mirror the skirt was still too short and the jacket proved it.

I sighed walking out of my room to see Shinta sitting on the couch seeming to be lost in thought; I took the chance to get him back for changing me while I was unconscious. I snuck up behind him and got ready to jump on him; he hadn't moved counting down in my head *3...2....1* I jumped on him. Right before I landed Shinta turned around and almost hit me with his katana, still in its sheath; he recognized me and looked shocked, stopping in his tracks holding out his arm to catch me. When I landed Shinta asked if I was alright.

"Yes, I'm fine" I realized my butt felt a little cold, but I ignored it thinking it was just my head playing tricks on me.

"Shi- Shinra-chan... Your- your skirt is up..." Shinta said looking away, turning red again.

I jumped up and fixed my skirt, my face feeling even redder than before "Uh... L-lets go eat..." I said scratching the back of my head.

"Ok. Um, do you know how to ride a horse?" Shinta said

leading the way out the door. "N-no" I couldn't look at Shinta, *That's the second time he has seen my underwear!* I thought to myself my face getting hotter. "It should be fine, you're riding with me. Just hold my waist and don't lean to one side too much, or you'll put Damutsui off balance... Damutsui is mama's mustang, he only just recently started letting me ride him, and hopefully he'll let you ride with me..." We just got out the door when he finished talking.

Dr. Kamimura was coming out towards us glaring at Shinta like he had committed the vilest crime on earth.

"Shinta, What are you planning?"

"I was going to get Shinra-chan some breakfast." Shinta replied to Dr. Kamimura casually. Then she held out her pinky smirking at him.

"Hizuke no yo na?" She said with a big grin on her face.

"IIE" Shinta replied quickly and annoyed. He gave her an evil look.

"Anata wa watashi no uma o totte i nai, migi o shitte iru." I was looking back and forth between the two of them, I was so confused, they were speaking gibberish I had no idea what they were saying, but it was funny to see Shinta so flustered.

"Come on Shinta." I said smiling "Let's go I can't wait to go outside these walls... Come on" I said cheerfully.

"Okay Shinra-chan" Shinta said smiling back.

"Yoi, Shinta shite." Dr. Kamimura said after Shinta had turned around to face me. He rolled his eyes at the comment.

"Does Mr. Kanasai have a car?" I thought we were going to ride a horse, but I answered his question anyway "Yes he does... Why?" Dr. Kamimura turned to walk away smiling like she was proud of something.

"Mama won't let us take Damutsui…"

Mama I thought to myself.

"Could you get the keys?" I smiled at Shinta like I was a mischievous child.

"I don't have to he keeps them in the visor."

Chapter Six: The Assumed Date

I led Shinta to Ikuto's car and I was right he left it unlocked and the keys were in the visor.

"Ikuto doesn't concern himself with safety too much." I sighed I wish he did though if he were concerned about safety for his belongings maybe he would care about my safety as well.

I tried to put it out of my mind, the way Ikuto looked at me yesterday when he came in; his eyes were so full of fear and he ran away. Shinta saw the look on my face and touched my shoulder I figured he was trying to comfort me as he tried to earlier and we all know how that turned out. I looked at Shinta and sighed again I was so embarrassed about the whole underwear incident and the fact he changed my clothes while I was unconscious, but he was only trying to help... *at least that's what he said.*

"So... Shinra-chan" he smiled at me sweetly "What would you like to eat this morning?" I looked down at the clock and saw that it said 11:30.

"Shinta... It's almost lunch time." He scratched the back of his head still smiling, but a more embarrassed kind and his cheeks were turning a little pink. "Oh... Heh-Heh oops."

He laughed a little and opened his eyes smiling again "In that case... Where do you want to go eat for lunch?" Shinta started the car and sat waiting for my answer. I thought about all the places I had never been and heard of.

"How about this place called McDonalds?" I looked down embarrassed "I have never been there and everyone says it's really good." He smiled at me with an even bigger smile.

"I love McDonald's... So McDonald's it is." Shinta put

the car in reverse and backed out of the parking space; I was finally leaving these grounds, after years of living on only the school grounds I couldn't wait to see what was on the other side of these gray boring walls I had grown so accustomed to.

"YAY!" I yelled almost bouncing out of my seat; Shinta put his arm across my chest trying to hold me still.

"Hey calm down a little it's not that exciting." He blushed as he looked out at the road.

"Why are you so excited?" He asked pulling his hand away from my chest.

"How can I not be excited?! I finally get to see the real world and interact with humans!" I was ecstatic I couldn't sit still.

"You have really never been outside the school's barrier... Have you?" he sounded sad at this fact so I smiled at him.

"Nope! But thanks to you I get to today... Ikuto would never bring me outside those damn barriers he says it's because people would stare at me ...." I looked down and saw two hats in the floor. "Shinta... What's with the hats?" I was confused as hell at this point.

"Those are to cover our ears" he said not looking at me "We can't exactly go walking around town with wolf and cat ears sticking out of our heads, now can we?" He smiled a little.

"Oh yeah" I pulled my ear "I forgot about those... Wait what about our tails?!" I grabbed my skinny white tail and blushed; my skirt was too short to hide it in. "Hmm... Well mine is easy to hide because I'm wearing pants, but yours is going to be tricky." he looked like he was really thinking hard about how to hide it. "You could put it in your.... underwear...." Shinta blushed heavily and watched the road more intensely; I blushed too and looked out the window.

"It's an idea..." He said aloud still blushing.

"Yes it is... But I don't want to lift my skirt in public to hide my tail..." I thought about what was another way I could hide it under my skirt, but the only thing that popped in my head was the idea Shinta had.

"O-ok I'll do it, but I'm doing it in the car." Shinta nodded.

"I won't look... I promise" His face was beet red and he stayed starring at the road; I lifted my skirt reluctantly and started to try and roll up my tail. I took frequent looks in Shinta's direction to make sure he kept his promise and he did; his face couldn't get any more red.

I put my tail in my underwear and pulled my skirt down quickly, it felt funny to have it rolled up and right against my skin; I grabbed the hat and put it on my head using the mirror to adjust it so it covered my ears all the way. I looked at Shinta and asked a very serious question blushing "H-how do I look?" He glanced over at me a few times and laughed. I pouted and looked away "D-do I look that bad?" He tried to stop laughing so he could answer me.

"No, no I'm laughing because you look like a normal human except for your eyes." He smiled at me "You look great Shinra-chan." I'm going to give him the biggest hug when we get out of this car; I handed Shinta his hat and he put it on. "Hey hold the wheel for a bit ok?" He held the wheel with one hand and looked at me.

"O-ok" I took the wheel and he unbuttoned his pants "Hey!" I let go and sat up straight in my seat; my face felt so hot I thought it was going to melt off! Shinta grabbed the wheel trying to get control of the car.

"I was trying to hide my tail!!" He looked over at me and gave me an *'are you stupid'* look.

"S-sorry..." I grabbed a hold of the wheel and steered for him as he unzipped his pants and tucked his tail away. I tried keeping my eyes on the road and I knew my face was still as red as before, it wouldn't be going away anytime soon; Shinta zipped his pants and buttoned them again, he took the wheel letting me get up and sit in my seat. There was a long silence Shinta and I just sat there quietly, we didn't even look at each other; after a while I started feeling silly about not talking to him because of *'that'*.

"S-so…" I said hesitantly messing with my fingers "W-what are you going to get at McDonald's?" My face still felt like it was on fire.

"O-oh.... Um... Probably a Big Mac..." he smiled a little.

"What's a Big Mac??" I looked at him confused; we were pulling up into a parking spot at a yellow and red building.

"Why are you covering your eyes Shinra-chan?" Shinta asked laughing to himself.

"It's just so bright" I said my eyes still covered.

"'Bright'? Oh, yeah, you would think that, you've only lived in that damp dull building..." Shinta said in response; I uncovered my eyes to look at Shinta.

"Shall we go in then?" I smiled innocently at him.

"Yep." Shinta said with a smile. It was then I noticed how cute he was. I looked away blushing a bright shade of red.

"O-ok" I stuttered; Shinta got out of the car and came around to my door opening it for me. "T-thanks." I knew my face was still bright red so I kept looking at the ground; Shinta lifted up my chin smiling.

"Head up. You'll look like you're hiding something." He saw my face and smiled sweetly, then turned to the door of McDonald's with his hands in his pocket; I followed him demanding my own face to go back to its original pale color before we got inside. I was amazed, there was a play area with little kids having fun, a waiting area for their parents and booths to eat in "wow"

"What the play-place?" Shinta asked turning around, his face seemed to light up. "When mama wasn't hounding me, papa and I would come to eat here and I'd play there for hours when I was younger." I looked at Shinta and smiled asking a very innocent question.

"Is there an age limit?"

"No... But you have to be less than five feet tall..." He said looking at me up and down; I gave him a big smile.

"I'm not too far over five foot... Can I go play in it Shinta?" I put my hands together like a child asking their parents for a pet kitten "Ple~ase"

Shinta smiled a little.

"Ok just order first." I knew my face lit up at that moment with a very big happy smile.

"Ok! Thank you Shinta!" I kissed his cheek and thought *CRAP! I shouldn't have done that*; I looked up at Shinta and my face felt on fire. I turned around hiding my face "I-I'll go order now."

"Ok." Shinta said lifting a corner of his lips in a cute smirk; I walked up to the counter Shinta following right behind me.

"C-could I have a Big Mac please?" Shinta stepped up beside me.

"And a chicken select." He said a smile on his face; the girl looked at us bored and non-affected by anything.

"I have a Big Mac and a Chicken Select... Anything else?" She asked bluntly; I shook my head.

"No ma'am."

"Ok it will be $7.76 please." the lady behind the counter said; Shinta reached for his wallet.

"Ok thank you." he replied. I looked down again.

"If I had any money I would pay for it..." I mumbled hoping

Shinta wouldn't hear me.

"Huh? Oh, No. You don't have to pay for it, I'm buying you lunch." Shinta said.

I looked up at him "Y-you heard that?" My face felt red again.

"Yeah, I hear everything." He leaned down closer and whispered near my ear "I have wolf ears..." I blushed brighter he was so close.

"I-I-I'm going to go play now..."

"Hehe, OK, have fun" He moved away from me and waited for the food; I turned and walked to the play area some people were staring at me but I ignored them to the best of my ability. A few of the kids that were there stared at me one even came up and pointed at my neck."You have a messy line across your neck" the little girl said; I put my hand to my neck realizing the collar wasn't on, I walked out and over to Shinta still covering my neck.

"What's wrong Shinra-chan?" Shinta asked then his face lit up "OH! Wait here." He ran out to Ikuto's car and came back with a blue ribbon in his hand; he handed it to me.

"Here I found this in the car. You can wear it; I think Ikuto had it in the glove box just in case." I took it and put it on sad he hadn't thought of it earlier.

"It's a little late for that... but thank you..." I looked down hiding my face from everyone else I knew they were staring at me and so did Shinta.

"...Sorry..." Shinta said then the lady behind the counter called out their order.

"We should probably get that..." I looked at the lady and she was staring at me just like everyone else, I looked back down and covered my neck where the ribbon was.

"Yeah." He turned around, grabbed the tray and walked

to one of the tables, looking back occasionally to check and make sure I was still following; Ikuto did that all the time like he was making sure I didn't run away.

"You mentioned your papa... what's he like?" I asked sitting down at the table.

"My papa? Well... He's a teacher at the academy, Mr. Kamimura. He teaches art." He said eating his food.

"He teaches art? He isn't a..." I pointed to his covered ears "You know starts with a 'W'..." I wasn't trying to be rude I just wanted to know.

"What's that supposed to mean? Wolves can be good at art too." He said with a snap in it, I could tell I touched a nerve.

"I didn't mean it like that..." I looked down at my food "Shinta... why did you keep looking back at me?"

Shinta gave me a confused look at first "Oh! It's a part of the wolf language, it's not all vocal you know..." He looked at his watch "You better hurry up 'n' eat your food with the size of your face." He chuckled to himself "We don't want to be late to Dr. Kamimura's class she will make us do laps!" he laughed and I noticed he was actually having fun. I took a few bites out of my burger and swallowed.

"What does it mean... when you look back at someone so much?"

"Huh? Oh... nothing..." he paused and looked at his watch again "Better hurry, we'll be late..."

I finished my burger and looked at him "Will you tell me what it means?"

"Maybe later. We have to leave now." He said in a hurried voice; so we got in Ikuto's car and this time Shinta drove like a maniac. He cut corners, he sped, he drifted like those guys in Tokyo Drift and yet I felt safe riding with him. By the time we got back to school grounds the warning bell was ringing.

"Do you have everything you need for mama's class?" Shinta asked throwing the car into park.

"Y-yes…" I stuttered still in shock from the car ride there.

"Good. Hop on my back, I'll carry you there." He got in a position for me to get on.

"B-b-but what about my skirt?" I blushed and thought *I don't know how Shinta would feel about touching my butt…*

"Hmmm" you could tell he was thinking; then he went around to the truck of the car and opened it, rummaging around through it. "Ah-ha!" he said pulling out a pair of jeans "Here, wear these… They may not fit, but they will cover your hinny for the time being. Hurry now or we'll be late!" I blushed brighter looking at the jeans.

"Here in the parking lot?" I looked at him "Fine…" I waited for Shinta to turn around.

"Just put them on under your skirt." He said as he turned around; I lifted my skirt and started to put on the pants looking over at Shinta occasionally making sure he wasn't looking

"There I'm done."

"Good now hop on my back, hurry." he knelt down again getting in a position for me to get on.

"What if I crush you?" I said looking down at him.

"Don't worry. Now come on before I throw you over my shoulder." He said in a hurry, I did as he said and reluctantly got on his back; he put his hands under my butt so I wouldn't fall.

"Alright, ready? Hold on." He didn't even give me a chance to answer he just bolted; I almost fell off when he started running, but I regained my grip and held on as tight as I could shutting my eyes so I wouldn't get to scared.

"C-choking…" he managed to get out still running at full speed; I loosened my grip enough so he could breathe easily and squeaked "S-sorry".

"Almost there." He said sliding around the corner, "Alright here we are." He sat me down on the floor."

"Now let's get in before the bell rings." He opened the door and let me in Dr. Kamimura looked over her glasses at us; Shinta walked in just as the bell rang "You're late." She said to Shinta motioning for me to sit down, the only two seats open were right in front of her desk in the front row. Shinta glared at her and Dr. Kamimura was giving him a disappointed look through her glasses

"Yes ma'am..." he said in a steady voice.

"Go sit down" she said "I can deal with you at home." I think I was the only person in the room that didn't say "OOOOH". Despite the embarrassment he walked to his desk with his head held as high as it always is.

"I'm sorry I got you into trouble..." I whispered as he sat down next to me.

"Don't be sorry she would only do that to me." He said in a whisper so soft I could barely hear him; when I looked back Dr. Kamimura was glaring at us from behind her desk, holding her attendance book.

"She is kinda scary..." I whispered looking back at Shinta "You said both your parents teach here?"

"Yeah" he answered "My papa, Mr. Kamimura, teaches Art and mama, Dr. Kamimura," he pointed to the teacher "Teaches World history and sword classes here at the academy."

"I bet you have a lot of fun" I smiled at him innocently; his answer was simply "Tch..." before Dr. Kamimura turned around and looked at us.

"Shinta, Tsuki, in the hallway. Now." She said harshly; I flinched at her voice she sounded mad and I mean real mad.

"Yes Ma'am" I squeaked and stood up from my seat

hurrying to the hallway; Shinta was cool and calm he stood up and walked over to the door saying "Yes ma'am".

She watched us walk out the door and followed; shut the door and turned with a smile on her face.

"So how did your date go?" she laughed a little; Shinta and I looked away from each other blushing.

"I-I-It wasn't a date mama!" he said crossing his arms; I blushed brighter and looked down at the ground, I was hoping he would consider it a date, but I shouldn't have gotten my hopes up.

"Y-yea… it wasn't a date…" I said trying to hide the sadness in my voice and face; Dr. Kamimura slapped Shinta on the top of the head.

"Admit it, you like her and it was a date." she said smiling and winking at me, I smiled back at her blushing brighter; Shinta rubbed his head and looked at me blushing heavily.

"F-fine…. Yes it was a date… and I kinda like you." He looked back at Dr. Kamimura "Happy?"

"Yes" She smiled at both of us "Now take a minute and get your faces back to normal." She said laughing going back into the room "Oh and you both have 50 laps for talking during class." We both looked at each other, and then at the floor "Yes Ma'am" Shinta and I said.

Chapter Seven: The Attack Begins

A few weeks passed, classes were on schedule and I wasn't making friends like I had hoped, but Shinta was still there so I had at least one friend; Shinta said there were more reports of demon attacks on the students. He decided that it would be a good idea to stay close to me so that he could protect me; the moon was so pretty out in the clear night sky.

"Shinta you really don't have to do this…" I said as I was riding on his shoulders "The whole point of a midnight stroll is to be alone."

"You are alone you're just dreaming me up." He said smiling.

"Oh really" I said as I pinched his cheek "You sure feel real." I laughed at the face he made.

"Ouch why do you hurt your imagination?" Shinta said jokingly, then his ear twitched and he went slightly serious, "Did you hear that?"

I sat up and listened to see if I could hear anything, but I couldn't.

"Hear what?" I asked concerned, I felt myself start to shiver; Shinta saved me twice after that first attack by the demon, I hoped he wouldn't have to do it again. Shinta changed into his saber form with me still on his shoulders, he was so tall it was scary being up this high; I was so scared I buried my face in his mane.

"Hold on tight, no matter what." He said getting serious; I held onto him tighter and nodded closing my eyes.

"Good girl" Shinta said and took off into the forest leaving the trail behind us; he suddenly stopped and sniffed the air. Even through Shinta's mane I could smell the graveyard soil;

I leaned against Shinta more raising my head, I was guessing the graveyard soil was what Shinta smelt.

"Shinta… D-do you smell graveyard soil too?" I asked nervously.

"Yes unfortunately…" Shinta looked back at me "Don't worry you're safe with me so stop shaking… it tickles" he looked forward again.

"Sorry…" I buried my face into his mane again trying to erase the scent of the demons.

"Shinta…"

"Nani?"

"What did you hear?…"

Shinta sighed at my question; "It sounded like an incantation…" he was walking through the forest again moving towards the source of the smell.

"Sorry, but I have to check it out… It's part of my job." I nodded and held onto him tighter; I could feel him breathe, every breath he took somehow seemed to calm me a little. We entered a clearing by the school wall and there was a man, he looked to be about twenty-one or maybe even younger; Shinta growled at him.

"Who are you and what is your business here?" Shinta asked, barring his teeth at the man; the man wasn't frightened of Shinta, but he seemed intent on looking at me.

"My name is Galidor it is a pleasure to make your acquaintance." He bowed his burning red eyes fixed on mine, I noticed as he bowed that there were two horns almost a foot long coming out of his violet colored hair; Shinta had not relaxed.

"Your business here?" Shinta asked growling; Galidor smiled.

"I heard there was a very special girl at this school…" His

eyes seemed to be analyzing me, "And I do believe you have brought her to me." Shinta stopped growling and looked back at me.

"How is she special to you...?" He cut his eyes back at Galidor.

"That is none of your concern mutt..." Galidor was still staring at me "But if the young lady asks I shall answer." His smile got bigger.

How could I be special, the only thing I have done my whole life is hide and heal people's wounds... That must be it! I can heal a wound that's why I'm special to him!

I held Shinta tighter, "I am of no use to you..." I said, but my voice cracked making him smile wider.

"So you are her and you know exactly what I'm talking about." Galidor took steps toward Shinta and me; I flinched accidentally pulling some of Shinta's hair, but he didn't react he bared his teeth at Galidor growling loudly, I could feel it rumble in his chest.

"I suggest you stop there." Shinta said his ears back defensively.

"Do you think I'm going to hurt her?" Galidor asked finally looking at Shinta; I patted his shoulder trying to calm him.

"If you aren't going to hurt her, what do you want her for?"

"What else I'm going to use her powers." Galidor said with an evil grin on his face; I slid off of Shinta's back and looked Galidor straight in the eyes.

"Shinra-chan I told you-"Shinta started to say, but he stopped, thinking about what Galidor had said, "What powers?" He looked at me confused.

"Galidor was it?"

"Yes" He looked pleased to hear my voice.

"How do you know about me... about my powers...?" I

stayed very close to Shinta.

"I was there 11 years ago. I saw you heal your own wounds, those disgusting wounds." Galidor looked at my throat "I see you have learned to hide the scar well." I immediately put my hand to my throat feeling the ribbon.

"It's too bad really… your blood has such a wonderful smell." A voice came from behind us. I looked to see who it was coming from; it was a boy with black hair spiked in the back and combed over in the front covering his right eye leaving his left brown eye in the open.

"W-who are you…?" I asked backing up a step, he smelled a little like something from my past, but I couldn't put my finger on it.

"Who me? Oh no one special, just the guy who is going to suck the life out of you; when Master is done playing with his new toy." Shinta turned around instantly and bared his teeth at the boy, but the boy didn't react.

"Stop scaring the girl Rath." I heard Galidor say he sounded like he was right behind me and I felt a hand on my shoulder gripping it tightly, "We don't want her running off now do we." Shinta swung his massive paw aiming at Galidor's head; he picked me up with the one hand and was almost crushing the bones in my shoulder with his grip. Shinta's attack passed right by my neck cutting the ribbon, but not me.

"Shinra-chan!" he looked at me apologetically.

"It's ok… It's ok…" I raised my usable hand "I-I'm f-…" I felt my shoulder blade break under Galidor's grip and I screamed in pain; the next thing I knew Rath was standing beside me and Shinta was growling loudly again posed for a strike.

"Oooh, do I get to have a taste?" Rath sounded giddy about the whole aspect; Shinta took a step forward he looked so angry.

"A taste of what!?"

"Well her of course. What else would I be tasting? A mutt like you?" Rath raised his eyebrows at Shinta "I doubt you would taste as good as her." I felt something scratch my arm and warm liquid ran down it "Let me go" I said trying to get away, Galidor only tightened his grip braking my shoulder blade more; I screamed again starting to cry "Shinta…" Shinta had been thinking of ways he could help me, he growled louder at the boy named Rath as he licked the blood from my arm; I couldn't stay awake the pain was leading to shock, I would be out cold soon and I had to do something.

"Shi-Shinta… Look away." I said readying myself for an extreme burst of energy from my hands.

"No, I won't give them the chance to take you." He argued, how come he always argues!

"They won't take me just look away!" I sent him a reassuring look, but he looked like he didn't believe it.

"Please Shinta… just trust me." I pleaded with him; he did close his eyes, but didn't turn his head.

"Galidor… Rath… I'm sorry about this." I shut my eyes and concentrated hard feeling the energy swirl around my hands, molding it into a weapon.

"Excuse me?" Galidor asked confused.

"Sorry?" Asked Rath; as soon as I had enough energy molded I positioned my hands one facing Rath, the other facing Galidor. I didn't want to hurt anyone, but I couldn't let them take me either; since my eyes were closed I didn't know Shinta was watching me.

"I'm sorry…" I said as I sent the energy at their midsections sending both of them backwards away from me; Galidor released my shoulder and when I hit the ground I put my hand to it energy still focused and healed the broken bones. Shinta was running towards me still in his saber form.

"Shinra-chan what… How did you…" He sighed calming himself "Are you ok?"

I smiled at him weakly "Fit… as… a fiddle" I said breathing heavily; he didn't have any enthusiasm in his eyes or in his voice.

"You should have stayed on my back like I told you to." He looked at the young Rath lying unconscious not twenty feet from us, Galidor had disappeared; I followed Shinta's gaze feeling sorry for Rath.

"I think… I over… did it…" I crawled over to Shinta "Take… me to him" I said; Shinta raised his eyebrows at me.

"I don't think so." He said moving away from Rath.

"Shinta please…" I pulled at his mane making him stop and look at me again; he looked at me concerned a little, but finally agreed to take me over to him.

"Thank you."

"Yeah yeah…" He looked away from me; I knelt down to Rath and looked at his wounds he had a severe burn on his chest where my energy had hit him. I concentrated again and made a bubble around Rath with my energy; I thought of healing and saw as his wounds starting to disappear as his eyes opened.

"W-what…" Rath looked at me and the bubble around him; he clawed at it, but it wouldn't break.

"Rath… If you keep… trying to break it… I won't be able… to heal you." I was exhausted I had never used this much energy in such a short amount of time; I saw him look at his chest and at the almost healed burn; he stopped fighting the bubble and looked at me amazed.

"You really can…" he smiled a little "Thank you Ms."

"My name… is Shinra and it's… no problem" Rath's wound

was healed and the bubble disappeared; my eyes would barely stay open "I... felt bad..." I said falling forward onto his lap passing out; I woke up on Ikuto's couch and Rath was sitting in a chair next to me.

"Hello there Ms. Shinra." He said with a smile on his face "How are you feeling?"

I smiled back at him "I knew you were a good person... I finally remembered your smell" He looked surprised, but then smiled sweetly at me "You do, do you?"

I nodded "I knew you when I was little... You were one of my best friends" Rath smiled bigger and rubbed my head "Oh yeah you were the little pip squeak that followed me around." He laughed at me.

"I did not... I just wanted to play with someone and you were always busy with your studies so I waited until you were done..." I smiled at him like I use to and he blushed scratching the back of his head.

"N-no more like you pestered me 'Are you done yet Rath?... Can you play now?' you followed me asking me that all the time." I giggled at Rath's face.

"You are blushing Rath." he covered his face quickly.

"No I'm not!" He got up and walked to the door "I have to go register for my classes..." and he left; Shinta came from the kitchen laughing.

"Well that was fun to watch." He said wiping his hands with a towel.

"He hasn't changed all that much..." I smiled looking at Shinta "How long was I out?"

Shinta looked down his smile gone "Three days..." he looked back up at me seriously "What were you thinking?"

"I was thinking Galidor didn't have a partner." I looked back at the door "I know why he was acting so strange...

Galidor can manipulate people with his energy." Shinta looked at me shocked.

"You could tell…" He said thinking to himself; I nodded.

"That's why I used more force on Galidor than Rath." I got up from the couch and walked over to him, "You think I'm weird now… don't you…?" Shinta looked at me funny.

"No… Interesting yes, weird no." he gave me a sweet smile and I felt my face turning red.

"I have tried to hide it from everyone…" I looked down at the ground "Ikuto even had to get use to my abilities… which reminds me where is he?" Just as I asked the question he came through the doors happy to see me awake. *Speak of the devil and he shall appear.*

"Shinra!" He hugged me, picking me up as he did.

"I-Ikuto?" I blushed brighter as Ikuto's head was right against my chest; he swung me around giggling.

"I-Ikuto… put me down… I'm going to throw up." Ikuto put me down and I ran to the sink throwing up whatever was in my stomach; Shinta pulled my hair out of my face so I wouldn't get anything in it.

"Thanks Shi-" I couldn't get anything else out because more of last night's meal came from my stomach and into the sink.

"Does this always happen when you use too much energy?" Shinta asked still holding my hair and started rubbing my back.

"Yea it has happened a few times before, but those were my fault…" Ikuto said looking down, "You said the guy's name was Galidor right?" Shinta nodded.

"I think I have heard his name somewhere before…" Shinta scratched his head and thought for some time as my stomach started to settle down. "I heard he was a powerful demon who preys on Tenshi like us and can control armies of lesser demons…" he said wrapping a blanket around me.

"You have heard right Shinta." Ikuto walked me over to the couch sitting next to me in the chair letting Shinta take the spot next to me on the couch, "He does indeed prey on Tenshi and likes to go for the younger ones who don't know how to defend themselves well." They both looked at me.

"Hey I defended myself." I said looking from Ikuto to Shinta, "Now will you guys stop moving" Shinta looked concerned and held up three fingers.

"Shinra-chan…. How many fingers do you see?" I pointed to each one counting.

"1…2…3…4…5…6… I see six." They both looked at me.

"We need to talk" they said at the same time and Shinta laid me across his lap stroking my hair; I eventually fell asleep about fifteen minutes after Shinta started stroking my hair.

Chapter Eight: Deceived

Almost a month passed since Galidor came to try and take me away, the attacks by demons were no longer random they were focused on me; Ikuto, Shinta, Dr. Kamimura, Mr. Kamimura and Dr. Uzayaki had come to an agreement on my situation.

"Since Mr. Kanasai, Dr. and Mr. Kamimura along with myself have students to attend to and business that needs our attention you shall move in with Shinta, so he can protect you if need be." Dr. Uzayaki said looking very serious, "You are to pack your things and move immediately." I blushed brightly looking at Shinta and then at Ikuto; Ikuto looked sad and turned away from me.

"Do you understand Ms. Tsuki?"

"Y-Yes ma'am."

"Do you understand Shinta?"

"Hai." Shinta held his head high as always and was serious as ever.

"Good now start packing." She left the room with Mr. Kamimura and Dr. Kamimura; Ikuto stayed behind to help me pack while Shinta waited by the door.

"I don't like this Shinra... I don't like this at all." Ikuto said handing me my clothes from the closet.

"I know I have a bad feeling too, like something bad is going to happen." I held the clothes close to my chest; there was a shirt and a pair of pants that belonged to Ikuto in the bundle of clothes.

"I'll be back before you know it..." I handed Ikuto one of my ribbons and he tied it around his wrist "You can keep it till I get back ok?" He pulled me into a hug and whispered in my ear so softly, but almost hissing.

"It's going to be hard to sleep... knowing you're alone with another guy." Ikuto looked me in the eyes and caressed my face coming very close to me; I stood completely still, I didn't know what to do. He leaned in closer his lips touched mine and my lips fit his perfectly; my eyes closed unwillingly as Ikuto kissed me more passionately his tongue softly licking my lips asking permission to open my mouth and let him in. I gasped softly as soon as my mouth opened his tongue found its way in; his scent began to change and morph. I pushed away from him looking in his eyes; Ikuto's eyes were now red.

"Shi-Shinta!" I fell backwards onto my butt and began to crawl away; Shinta came running in with his sword drawn.

"Shinra-chan what is it?!" He said looking at my terrified face; I pointed at what used to be Ikuto, he had turned into Galidor and was smiling at me.

"Well you do taste wonderful." Galidor licked his lips and chuckled at me as I blushed heavily and turned away from him.

"YOU!" Shinta growled "You're despicable!" Shinta roared and Galidor just laughed at him.

"I told you I was going to take her..." He smiled at me "And I was so close... What gave me away?"

"Your stench..." I hissed at him sounding cold "It seeped through Ikuto's." Galidor pretended to sulk and stuck out his bottom lip.

"Well I'll just have to try harder next time won't I?"

"Why do you want her so bad?" Shinta looked at me and Galidor smiled licking his lips once more "Why don't you?" Galidor disappeared from the room and Shinta's face was a slight pink color as he looked at me.

"Shinta?" He looked away from me, "Hey don't look

away..." I caressed his face so he had to look at me.

"Shinta will you promise me something?"

"Nani?"

"Promise me you won't ever leave..." I felt my cheeks warm up slightly at my own words; Shinta raised an eyebrow at me and smiled sweetly.

"I promise I will never leave you Shinra-chan."

I hugged Shinta tightly "Thank you…" I said being happier than I ever have been.

I gathered my clothes from the floor and stood up waiting for Shinta to lead the way to his room; he took my arm softly with one hand and started to lead me out of the room.

"Shinta I'm kinda tired when we get to your room can I take a nap?" we were walking down a corridor when I looked out the windows and smiled seeing the way the sky looked at twilight, the purples, the reds, and the pinks, even some lavender colors, it was so pretty.

"Sure you can… Hey what are you looking at?" he said his voice sounding curious as he looked off to where I was staring.

"The sky… it's so colorful I have never seen it look so wonderful." Shinta chuckled at me as he watched my expression.

"Your face looks so cute Shinra-chan." He smiled happily at me and I felt my cheeks turn a little red and smiled back like a child.

"Hehe thanks." I looked back down the corridor and saw a large door with something around its frame, as we got closer I was able to see little carvings of wolves all over the wooden frame.

"Here we are; my home sweet home." He sounded proud to say it the smile on his face was so cute and happy.

"The carvings are so cool." I ran my fingers over them as Shinta opened the door to his room.

"Dr. Uzayaki has each door made especially for the people who live inside the rooms." He said as he walked into the room leading me inside by my arm; I looked at the room and saw how big it was, I was so amazed it was so comfy looking. I saw the couch and laid down on it almost immediately snuggling up to a pillow that was there; Shinta smiled at me putting a blanket over me and pet my head.

"Shinta… thank you for protecting me and dealing with me like this…" I closed my eyes sleepily and heard him chuckle at me.

"I'm not dealing with you… I'm doing this because you are my friend and I care for you." His voice faded away as my mind faded into darkness.

Chapter Nine: The Battle

I awoke to sheets being pulled away and stirring beside me; I rubbed my eyes as I opened them trying to adjust them to the light coming down on me from the window above my head.

"Nyaaaa bright..." pulling the covers back over to me and over my head I curled up.

"Shinra-chan you awake?" I heard Shinta's voice say; I turned over to look at him as he lay there next to me.

"Shinta... why are you in my bed?" I asked tiredly stretching.

"Shinra this is my bed..." He said smiling at me as he sat up getting out of the bed, stretching as he stood up, "Do you not remember when you came to me last night?" I shook my head no blushing lightly trying to remember.

"Will you tell me what happened?" I asked hitting a road block in my own memory.

"Of course I will." He said smiling softly at me, "You came to me afraid, trembling, and crying... You asked if you could lay with me because you were afraid of thunder I tried to make you feel better, but you ended up crying yourself to sleep... I did make you a promise though and I swear to keep it at any coast." Shinta smiled at me with a sincere look in his bright blue eyes; I sat there blushing at his words and heard his voice in my head, *"I promise... I won't let anything hurt you..."* I smiled to myself hearing the promise again in my head. Shinta took my hand and helped me out of the bed; he led me to the couch and sat me down his smile still soft.

"What would you like to-..." He said turning around, but his sentence was stopped as Dr. Kamimura ran into Shinta's room; I flinched at the sound of the door crashing in.

"Shinta follow me quickly! We have bad company on the grounds!"

"Yes ma'am." I got up as well and started to follow Mrs. Kamimura "I'm coming too"

"No!" she said fairly harshly "It's too dangerous. You need to stay here."

"Yeah" Shinta said reinforcing his mother's words "You need to stay here." he said squeezing my shoulders.

"But i can help…" I looked back at Shinta "You know I can help you saw me the other day…"

"Yes, but I don't want you to get hurt." I could tell from his voice he was very concerned about me and wanted me to stay safe.

"He's right Shinra-chan." Mrs. Kamimura replied "I usually keep medical people hidden and away from the battle field. I can't risk you getting hurt… If I did Shinta would never let me hear the end of it." She said trying to make me smile.

"But I can fight too; I made Galidor go away the other day, didn't I?" I said in a pleading voice "Please I can help…"

"He just likes you…" Mrs. Kamimura said "You could get him to do a lot of things..." I sat back down and looked at my hands.

"Alright I'll stay here..." I said defeated.

"Thank you Shinra-chan." Shinta said, relived, finally letting go of my shoulders.

"Let's go!" Mrs. Kamimura cried, running out the door, and Shinta fallowed shortly after, giving me one more, quick, look; I smiled at him sweetly to give him some comfort "Come back safe Shinta..."

"Always do." He shouted back at me as he ran out the door; I looked at my hands again and sighed.

"I'm not just going to sit here though..." I said to myself;

I waited for about five minutes to give Shinta a head start and left the room heading to the grounds. I ran onto the lawn hearing growls and screaming; I looked around for Mrs. Kamimura and Shinta but couldn't see them. Instead, I saw demons attacking teachers and people running away, fleeing into Ranson's academy for protection. Finally, I saw her; she was fighting one of the bigger demons back to back with the principal right behind her, fighting another of the bigger demons. I ran towards them, but a demon grabbed my arm pulling me away

"Let go!" I screamed, but the demon didn't respond and gripped my wrist tighter; suddenly my eyes found Shinta, he was busy with his own opponent, but he still yelled out.

"Mama! Obake! Anata gata no uchi no hitori wa, Shinra o tasukeru koto wa dekimasu ka?"

"I said let me go!" I hit his wrist with one energy burst and as he wailed letting go of me and I fell backwards on my butt; I was wondering what Shinta had said, but at the moment I didn't care.

"You ok Shinra-chan?!" he called out looking at me; I waved at him smiling.

"I'm fine! Pay attention to your own opponent!" I yelled at him averting my attention from the demon in front of me; at that very moment I diverted my attention, that demon tried to attack again; as he did Dr. Kamimura ran towards me.

"Obake! Tsugi no nitsu no sewa o suru koto wa dekimasu ka?!"

"Anata ga shite, Ran watashi o korosu tsumorida!" Replied Dr. Uzayaki, *why did they always talk in a language I couldn't understand when I am around?! It is always so frustrating!* I turned back to the demon my hands making a triangle as I concentrated.

"I said back off ugly!" a bright green barrier appeared in front of me and the demon hit it, but didn't break it instead it repelled his attacks.

"Will you guys trust me for just one second?!" I yelled at Dr. Kamimura, Dr. Uzayaki and Shinta.

"That will only keep them away for so long..." Dr. Kamimura said while walking over to the crazed, infuriated demon "...They need to be exterminated." she continued as she sliced through the demon's neck with her katana; it was an amazing sword. The handle was dark blue and the blade had carvings of wolves in it, also colored in with a very dark, almost navy, blue.

"I can do that too." I said pouting and releasing the barrier "Is anyone hurt? I came to help you guys, but i didn't know this many people would be fighting..." I looked around the grounds seeing demon after demon fall, but more just kept coming; it was like someone was showing every demon in the state where we were.

I got up from the ground patting the dust off my pants and looked back at Shinta concerned "You get hurt and I'll kick your butt..."

"Tch, Yeah, right." Shinta replied sarcastically as he stabbed a demon where its heart would be, if it had one, and sliced straight through its chest. I smiled at him sweetly and started running to the edge of the grounds, near the wall, and looked for any of the injured, anyone who needed help.

When Dr. Kamimura finally got to me, she wouldn't leave my side fighting off every demon no matter how big or small. I healed as many people as I could as fast as I could; guarding Dr. Kamimura's back if needed when a demon tried to hit her from behind. Every time I did, no matter how tied up she was, she always thanked me; I kind of wondered if it was where

Shinta got it from, he was so polite most of the time. I put up one large barrier around Dr. Kamimura, myself and a wounded girl to give her a break; she must have been exhausted or at least a little tired, i know i would have been.

"Dr. Kamimura... Thank you very much for protecting me..." I felt my cheeks turn a little pink with my small embarrassment.

"It's no problem" She replied swatting a few pixie sized demons to the ground killing them instantly. I healed the girls wound and she said thanks leaving the barrier; I heard a scream that sounded like Rath and I sprinted as fast as I could in his direction.

"SHINRA-CHAN!" Dr. Kamimura called after me "Wait!" she ran after me to catch up slashing demons down left and right.I rushed through the trees and accidently left her behind as I came to a gruesome scene; Rath was lying on the ground covered in blood and he wasn't moving; finally Dr. Kamimura caught up to me and looked at Rath.

"What happened to it?"

"I don't know, but I have to stop his bleeding quickly." I formed a bubble around him and started concentrating as I tried to heal his wounds.

"Dr. Kamimura things are fine here I'll put up a secondary barrier around me, go help Shintaplease." I said looking at her smiling; she took one more look me, then at Rath and ran out toward the melee and howled a howl that sent shivers down my spine, and probably everyone else's'. I put up the barrier and focused hard on Rath trying to heal his wounds but they wouldn't close.

"Why isn't this working...? Why isn't this....?" My barrier suddenly vanished, "What's going on?" I put up another barrier and saw that Rath's wounds had seemed to be closed;

I dissolved the barrier around him and came closer to him laying his head on my lap until he woke up. Rath slowly began to wake up and he looked up at me smiling.

"Hi." he said happily as he sat up giving me a warm hug and I hugged him back happily.

"I'm so happy you're ok." Rath hugged me tighter; I heard a strange noise, like a knife being drawn, and something cold seemed to be pressed against my neck.

"W-what are you doing?"

"I'm taking you with me." Rath said looking in my eyes the knife's cold blade placed hard against my skin.

"R-Rath why are you..." I heard rustling in the bushes and looked to the side to see if anyone came out, but no one did. Rath put my arm forcefully behind my back and kept the knife firmly against my skin.

"S-stop this Rath please…" A voice came from behind me it wasn't Rath's voice but I knew who it was.

"Hello again... little kitten I told you I would try harder."

"G-Galidor..."

Shinta rushed onto the scene with his hand on the hilt of his sword and in a fighting stance, he yelled at Galidor to let me go.

"Oh and why should I?" Galidor smiled slyly "I hold all the cards here…" He pressed the knife against my neck harder causing a small cut that started to bleed.

"Ow..." I said wincing at the slight pain and looked at Shinta sadly. At that very moment a wolf came out of nowhere from behind me biting Galidor's arm, making him drop the knife and call out in pain. A strange sensation began to come over me like my body was going numb and my legs started to move on their own.

"W-what's going on...?" Galidor smiled and made two of

his fingers look like a gun barrel.

"Got you." he said then placed the make-shift gun between the wolf's eyes and a blue light formed around his fingertips turning into a buzzing lighting.

"R-Run away!" I screamed at the wolf.

The wolf jumped away toward Shinta and turned in to Dr. Kamimura; Galidor laughed and his eyes seemed to burn with fire as he looked at Dr. Kamimura and Shinta.

"I told you! I hold all the cards!" Galidor was about to send the lightning at the both and with as much strength as i could muster i put up the strongest barrier making the lightning bounce around inside the Barrier hitting me, but Galidor absorbed the lightning like it was nothing

"SHINRA!" someone yelled, but I didn't know who.

"SHINRA-CHAN LET DOWN THE FEILD" the other yelled "I want to kill him now!"

My arms wouldn't move I couldn't control my power anymore, Galidor smiled at me.

"Now you're mine." I looked at Shinta and Dr. Kamimura I felt like I was betraying them; I mouthed "I can't" to them as tears started to roll down my face.

Dr. Kamimura had gotten very impatient and drew her sword quickly at the barrier; as she swung her sword the barrier broke. *Why did it do that?* I was taking a second look at her sword when I noticed it looked like it was made of lightning. *That must have been how!*

I collapsed to ground exhausted feeling something catch me; I felt like I was floating as I opened my eyes and saw I wasn't on the ground and something's arm was around waist. Then right be for me Dr. Kamimura lunged at Galidor, turning back into a wolf, aiming at his throat with her massive paw. Galidor Maneuvered around Dr. Kamimura's paw and wings grew from his back as he flew up to where I was being held by his minion in the sky.

All Dr. Kamimura could do was growl, she seemed so pissed; Dr. Uzayaki came running up, assessing the situation and jumped at Galidor and swung at him with her sword as it glowed so brightly in the moonlight leaving a big ugly cut across his chest.Galidor grabbed at his chest sending an evil glare at Dr. Uzayaki as he commanded the demon holding me to call off all the other demons "We have what we came for..." Rath and Ikuto came running from the other side of the campus looking up at me. Both times i was tricked. I felt tears running down my face as the scene before me got darker and blurry; I used a small amount of my energy to make a small crystalline star with red, blue, green, and white colored crystals for each point and dropped it wishing Galidor would leave me alone and let me stay. Galidor looked at me and seemed worried somehow.

"You look sick..."

"You are...the... sick... one..." I said exhausted and my sight went black as i passed out hoping Rath or Shinta had found my star.

Chapter Ten: Kidnapped

I felt something soft under my hands and against my legs it felt so nice, so cool against my skin; I turned onto my side the cool feeling moving to different parts of my legs and arms.

"Are you awake?" A man's voice said softly, but almost cold sounding in a way; I opened my eyes slightly, a light stinging them. I winced at the stinging sensation and looked at the man by my bed side; the man had pitch black hair and red eyes, they seemed almost gorgeous with the light from the lamp reflecting in them.

"W-where am I?" I said as my head began to ache like never before my hand went to my forehead hoping that it would stop the pain "Who are you?... Where's Rath...?" My mind was filled with the pictures of Rath's motionless body and I sat up immediately, trying to get out of the bed I had been placed in "Rath! I have to..." My legs were numb as soon as they hit the cold tile floor; the man caught me as my legs collapsed and placed me back in bed.

"Calm down... just relax." The man's voice was soothing and calm; I looked up in his eyes as he looked down at me.

"Who... are you?" I said weakly and confused; *why was I here? Where is Dr. Kamimura...? How are Rath and Shinta?* These were all questions I was asking myself as I looked up dazed at the ceiling.

"My name is Jerammy and I will be keeping an eye on you from now on." He said formally and handed me a bowl of warm beef stew "You must be hungry after all that time of sleeping." I smiled at him a little nodding my head as my stomach growled.

"Mr. Jerammy... What time is it?" I rubbed my eyes sleepily as I took the bowl; it was so warm against my fingertips almost scolding if I held it too long.

"It is four in the afternoon... You have been asleep nearly

five days. Are you sick?" He asked putting his palm to my forehead looking for a fever.

"No I'm not sick... Just very exhausted,Gali...dor..." I looked down at the bowl following the rim with my finger "Is this Galidor's castle?" I looked at Jerammy as I asked, "How did I get here?" Jerammy looked at me with an eyebrow raised in confusion.

"Didn't you come here on your own?" I shook my head no and looked back at the bowl putting it back on the bedside table, "So... How did you get here?" he asked looking at me.

"I... I don't... Remember..." Flashes of the battle flooded my head as I thought back trying to remember, "There was a battle and... And I was helping..." I threw the sheets off me and went to jump off the bed ready to run to the door.

"Miss don't you'll-" as my foot hit the floor immense pain shot through my body as I collapsed to the ground, screaming, and gripping my leg trembling in sheer agony.

"Ow~..." Trying to find any broken bones in my leg I softly pressed on spots where the pain was worse than anywhere else; hitting those spots felt like a white hot iron rod being pressed against my bone, muscles, and skin, as if it were burning a hole through my leg. Jerammy held out his hand to help me back into bed.

"I told you not to get up." He said, almost sounding like a growl as he put the covers back over me, "I was about to tell you it was broken."

"I-I'm sorry..." I said sadly, *I didn't mean to make him mad*, "I was going to find Galidor and ask if he made the demons leave Ranson's Academy..."

"Ranson's? You mean the school for young Tenshi?" Jerammy asked sounding surprised and curious at the same time; I nodded in response and put my hands on my leg, softly, forming a light green bubble around it, I winced at the pain as the bones reset and healed properly.

"What is that?" He asked looking at the bubble.

"It's a special... 'Gift' of mine... I can heal any wound..." My breathing was heavy as I slowly healed the breaks, to reduce the pain.

"How can you do that?" He seemed intrigued at my strange power, like he was seeing something like this for the first time.

"I guess you could say I was born with it..." my cat ears slightly perked at the memories of my mom's smile and my dad's laugh; the bones finally healed and I dispersed the bubble sighing in nervous anticipation. I softly put my foot on the floor and no pain resonated from the healed bones like the break never happened; smiling childishly proud of myself I looked at Jerammy, "It comes in pretty handy hehe."

"Apparently it does." He said smiling back softly, it was almost unnoticeable; Jerammy seemed a lot like Galidor, sure his manners weren't perfect, but he seemed like a very kind person. He also, somehow, seemed cold, like he wanted to keep a wall up guarding him from everyone else. The door to the room opened and a familiar purple head walked into the room looking at Jerammy with a stern look; Jerammy bowed and walked out the room leaving me and Galidor alone in this now cold room. He sat on the bed beside me and looked in my eyes, his burning red eyes staring mine light green ones down.

"I have a question for you and it is very important that you answer me."

"What is your question?" I asked timidly; he leaned in close his face inches from mine.

"Will you be my bride?" he asked seriously, not faltering, I looked in his eyes my own eyes widening at his question. *Be Galidor's bride?*

Would you like to see your manuscript become a book?

If you are interested in becoming a PublishAmerica author, please submit your manuscript for possible publication to us at:

acquisitions@publishamerica.com

You may also mail in your manuscript to:

**PublishAmerica
PO Box 151
Frederick, MD 21705**

We also offer free graphics for Children's Picture Books!

---

www.publishamerica.com

CPSIA information can be obtained at www.ICGtesting.com
Printed in the USA
BVOW04s1005180614

356728BV00001B/63/P